Astronomical Approach

By Jayceon Harris

2019.

First Printing: 2019

ISBN: 9781081585952

Jayceon Harris
astronomicalapproach@gmail.com

Ordering Information:

Special discounts are available on quantity purchases by corporations, associations, educators, and others. For details, contact the publisher at the above listed address.

U.S. trade bookstores and wholesalers: Please contact Jayceon Harris, email astronomicalapproach@gmail.com

note to reader

start the project
start the book
start the album
start the painting
start the podcast
start the conversation

I did, and this piece is a product of just starting.
I had no idea that it would eventually be this.

I consistently wondered if I would publish it,

or

how well it would do,
but I had a **relentless belief in myself despite evidence to the contrary.**

make sure you have it too.

<u>note to reader II</u>

It doesn't have to work—its poetry.

my poetry.
my outlet.
my relief.

Preface

August 15, 2018

I don't know when this
literary masterpiece,

If I do say so myself,

will be completed,
but I know that it won't be for a while

Get mother fucking ready!

Acknowledgements

I actually prepared this speech for the Grammys, but this came first.

Over the past two years, I have been conjuring up these words to share with all of you.

Yes, it took two years to write, but I had to recollect nearly 20 years of damage.

With that being said, thank you to everyone alluded to in here. You have given me one hell of a story when I walk up to get that Grammy.

Thank you to my editors, Leah and Kineta, for helping me perfect these words. Also, a huge shoutout to Jai for sharing her words with the world as well. I appreciate you all.

Lastly, I want to thank myself.
Continue to do great things.

Stay dangerous.

everyday I live on this Earth
I know that I become more
and more prepared for the next day

mentally,
physically,

and, **most importantly**,

emotionally.

Food for thought #1

the most beautiful things in the universe:

babies, smiling, laughing, mirrors, and black people in yellow

• • •

Food for thought #2

note to myself:

stop disengaging yourself because they resemble something you want to be.

look. listen. take in. grow.

with this mentality, one day you will be in a similar position.

"There exists an area so unfathomably large that humans refer to it simply as 'space'".

Unknown

mom,
dad,
friends,
and
enemies

my earthly possessions and thoughts can't explain
my true understanding of you all.

so here, I give you **An Astronomical Approach**.

welcome to space.

my dark thoughts aren't ready to be shared.

Milky Way

"By the sweat of your face, you shall eat bread till you return to the ground, for out of it you were taken; for you are dust, and to dust you shall return"

God, Genesis 3:19

stabilizer. connecter. believer.

when the stars did not shine bright enough,
your light protected me.

for that, I say thank you.

• • •

you have not had the life you have always wanted.

worrying about
the Earth,
the Stars,
and the unnamed celestial bodies,

you have had to forget about the Black Hole at
the center of your life.

As you eventually come to an unfortunate end,

I hope that you have had the chance to learn a
few things about the world

you had no planets and moons of your own—
you had to take care of everyone else's terrain.

enjoyable? no.
respectable? yes.

kindness is all too natural for you.

self-care is the best care.
self-love is the best love.
self-respect is the best respect.

-says everyone that doesn't do any of that.

the Earth has not given you the time of day.

the Earth has not allowed us to have
communication.

the Earth has not given you the credit you
deserve.

the power has been in the Earth's hand to change
the way the planets you governed were
structured, but it kept that power for itself.

we all know there will be a day the Milky Way will
be gone.

I struggle to even imagine what it will be like
when your support and gravitational pull is no
longer there.

it will be hell.

the Black Hole has finally run its course.
you have run yours as well.

it has been a great journey.

not a single body can say that you didn't show the
rest of us what a true galaxy was meant to do.

as the time dwindles away,
you have left your mark on my heart.

tears will run down my eyes as you leave our lives.

I do not know when, but when it does,
the Earth's heavens will be gaining a saint,
and all hell will freeze over.

you won't have the opportunity to shed tears at my funeral, so I let my guard down and poured a few for you.

i'll love you to the moon back.

the light you have given to this dark universe will travel to the ends of it until it is filled with only light.

Sun and Moon

"Three things cannot be hidden: the sun, the moon, and the truth"

Buddha

i’m sorry.

I put a time limit on your life span with me.

it has now been switched and replaced with a shorter one because the Moon has come into my life.

it taught me how to float in this world with them.

as the Moon and the Sun started to eclipse,
only my shadow was left.

from that point on, both of your life spans were shortened to compensate for my lack of love and respect for myself.

I am sorry that this adjustment in love had to be given through the medium of text, but my eyes and heart could not take the downpour of feelings it would experience if I spoke these words from my mouth.

• • •

choosing to let my actions speak for my words,
I tell you this.

hopefully, as we approach the Earth, Mars, and Uranus you both will start to understand why I chose to do this.

thank you for balancing me out,

both of you,

but the Earth has to learn how to deal with your relationship with one another.

continue to eclipse, and I will continue to work
on understanding my place in your solar and
lunar cycles.

even though all of that was said.

my love for you both is infinite.
no storm or apocalypse could change that.

as we progress into remarkable bodies.

I will always remember the times we shared to get
us here.

The laughs. The cries. And the falls.

Stars

"She says nothing at all, but simply stares upward into the dark sky and watches, with sad eyes, the slow dance of the infinite stars"

Neil Gailman (Stardust)

disclaimer:

these are feelings and thoughts expressed on paper
I still have love for you both.

if there is an issue, let's talk about it.
don't cancel me like you have in the past.

Hot and Cold by Jai Madelyn

there is a warmth that is present

always radiating to reveal an ambience of closeness
you'll always be drawn to this warmth,
always want to know more about it
called by it,
never able to truly experience it because it is its
potential that is most noticeable

it burns bright,
but also fast

the flame that is often seen doesn't seem to last
there is a coldness that is hidden
a chilling disposition that fails to hide itself when
most needed

an uncontrolled instinct that still refuses to be
satisfied by the pleasantness that the warmth provides
they are unable to coexist,
one always leads, the other follows

unsteady circumstances cause them to come out to
play
the frigidity does not want to go away

so there is **hot and cold**

one never seems to do what it is told
but they are balance…
to be continued

stars are peculiar.

we have no true understanding of them. we only truly know how they progress and that they are hot!

even the coolest of stars will singe your skin to mere dust particles.

Food for thought #3

you knew what the world did to me and you still
let it happen to me.

you call it self-pity, but I call it letting you know
that you fucked up my life.

period.
point.
blank.

no hard feelings, *right*?

wanting

I wanted to touch the stars.
when I got close to them

they burned me.
they singed me.
they marked me.

from afar, it was just what I wanted.
up close, they destroyed me from the outside in.

Food for thought #4

the lesser of two evils:

a mom fighting internally with herself

or

a dad fighting against his wife.

Food for thought #5

I can't wait to have kids to raise them
how I should have been raised.

sorry not sorry.

to my shining stars:

I'm struggling to get the words out because I know your rebuttal will be swift and brutal.

being aware of the truth hurts even more when you have to tell another who thinks of you as perfect.

i'm sorry, but listen!

-shut up!

• • •

perfection is not the name of this game—
I have grown up trying to be that way.

respect my efforts to acknowledge my
imperfections.

• • •

Please don't let me continue to lie to myself,
it hurts

reality check

Jayceon,

it's time to grow up. you don't have parents anymore.

June 1, 2019 at 1:12 am

a letter to my mom written June 1, 2019 at 1:00 AM

Hey Mom,

Since I have been home, I have been conflicted to have conversations with you. Not the 2 Broke Girls and Wendy Williams conversations, but the ones on the status of our relationship. Being away from the home for two years have been the best two years of my life. Yes, I have lost financial aid, been depressed, and have several rough nights, but knowing that I could grow and soar on my own was great.

We are very close, but very distant at the same time. Laughing over television shows and talking about your co-workers is fun and all, but when it is time to analyze our lives, you leave me to overthink by myself. Since going to counseling, I have some time to look over my life dynamics. As much as I cherish you, you have been a major piece in my hindrance towards certain things in my life. Not only that, your ability to not be open to understanding the toxic qualities of our relationship has caused me to become disengaged. Disengaged as in I have to set boundaries and expect for our relationship to never reach its highest potential due to our dynamics as a mother and son.

I know you constantly state that I am debating with you, and I'm not. I am just trying to let you know how I feel in hopes of it getting better. You seem to be disinterested from it all, and I cannot continue to feed into a relationship that has no hope of flourishing. It has been sad to know that I have had to cap the relationship with my father, but to know that my mother's end is coming soon is very saddening. You have a lot of trauma you have to deal with, and I have tried to be there to help you as much as I can, but, unfortunately, I cannot.

As the rest of the summer continues, I will get a job and situate my finances. After this summer, I will not be living with you for the continuation of my life. I think that we are great—where we are. If we continue on this path, we will not talk when I get a partner and have kids, and do all of that other adult stuff. This relationship may not be what I want it to be, but I hope that, soon, you are able to understand where I'm coming from after you do some soul searching.

You are strong and resilient, but at what cost to the people around you? Your growth was someone else's demise. Continue to work hard to keep things afloat. Anytime you want to start to build again, let me know; I'm always ready to build.

Your favorite black son (your only black son),

Jayceon

reality check over.
she never saw this.

I was a guest in your home
but I never had a room.

you have been tired of my existence since birth and you bringing me through to adulthood does not negate that you have always had this feeling towards me.

I have been your ball and chain. I am now letting you free, but you will always have that impression of me on your ankle.

remember that. **both of you.**

things that scare me

windows
doors
doorbells
knocking
keys jingling

all the things that scare me are the same things
that make up a house.

my home has only reminded me of the things that
break me down inside.

coming to terms that reality can break the heart
and leave the eyes watery.

oops, another reality check

my mother and father say to me,
"take responsibility for your actions"

I respond,
"I'll start when you do"

reality check II

my mother is depressed
my father is clueless
my sisters are broken
my brothers are unaware
my friends are unknowledgeable
my family is preoccupied

and I have to be okay with that.

stars are supposed to shine.
shine bright.

• • •

you have shined, but your immense
brightness has only blinded me.

but I can finally see again.

Hot and Cold by Jai Madelyn

continued

...the kind warmth provides the love that is needed
the coolness gives way, and to the warmth, it has heeded

then exists hot and cold in an atmosphere where love prevails and fear escapes
a collision of fire with ice begins to shape
cold evaporates and the hot waves are now the form
the warmth overcomes the atmosphere, and once again the coolness is hidden

now lies hot and cold, attempting to meet again

jai, continue to share your words with the world. it needs it.

Mercury and Venus

To my knowledge, I have not examined your terrain. Instead of theorizing what you could be, I will wait.

please be good to me.

Earth

a letter from myself to myself

"Let us preserve and increase this beauty"

Yuri Gargarin

the Earth has been me. always me.

• • •

you are the Earth.

you have issues, but you are in denial of them.

you have natural beauty,
but you don't give yourself enough credit.

you have so much to give.

not only to yourself, but the Universe.

even though your time is short,
give yourself the credit you deserve.

you spend too much time worrying about the
wrong things.

through this process. may you grow and blossom
into the true body you are.

speaking to myself in this piece,
I present to you…

the true Jayceon.

first of all, get hip to yourself, fam.

• • •

to begin, your beauty is unmatched.

you may not think that you are conventionally cute,

but you are conventionally **that nigga**.

lol, do white people say "nigga" in their head?!

probably, smh (shaking my head, lol)

<u>Food for thought #6</u>

I don't know if you are, but I will help you to be.

your strength and beauty are unmatched.

you often wait for someone to come and
compliment your wit and kindness, but you have
to compliment yourself.

• • •

continue to have hilarious conversations with
yourself.

continue to cry to yourself.

continue to sing Jazmine Sullivan to yourself.

you've been through hell and high waters;
you deserve it.

you aren't scared of lions, tigers, and bears
but you are afraid of spiders, commitment, and
being loved.

you know that,
and you are progressing and working on it.

I am going to keep my time short because we will have a long time to explore ourselves.

I am so honored to live the life I have.

being a different person would not have allowed me to meet the same people, deal with the same bullshit, and celebrate the little victories.

you did not elaborate because you know what you are capable of and what greatness you bring to this world, and what greatness you will soon give to the world.

one day you will have the platform to share your story with everybody in the universe,

but for now,

continue to impact every single person you meet today

once again,
stay dangerous.

"You are everything you are in search for"

-my future TED Talk

Mars

"Mars tugs at the human imagination like no other planet. With a force mightier than gravity, it attracts the eye to the shimmering red presence in the clear night sky"

John Noble

this journey has shown me that I am not the person I want to be.

I have failed and not gotten back up.
I have hurt and have not healed.
I have cursed but I have not replenished my blessing.

I have taken myself to depths never sought out.

I have become a person that I would never want
another to know about.

often, I forget if I'm writing this for

you or myself

the answer is

both

hopefully you can relate and I can recover.

life lesson 1

grown up tasks aren't fun
but once you do it
you'll get used to it.

• • •

life lesson 2

we all say the same thing.
what differs is how we hear it.

• • •

life lesson 3

pain will shoot you in the back.
faith will catch you as you fall forward.

-end of life lessons

I pray for a person who has lived through the struggle.

I also pray for the person who has not.

don't reduce my experience.
don't shadow my experience.
don't relate to my experience.
don't show sympathy to my experience.
don't cry at my experience.
don't (fill in the blank) at my experience.

just listen.

and don't rub my back, **I don't like that shit.**

I know that I am struggling, and I'm in some deep shit, but can we please acknowledge how far I've come and where I'm going.

i'm finally understanding that I am not healthy, and I need to do better. and I am doing better.

I am finally understanding that I need a relationship with God, and I am trying.

please, I am at a low in my life. can we just praise my growth in some area? that is what is keeping me afloat.

let's recognize that.

<u>Food for thought #7</u>

let me define my own terms.

Food for thought #8

everything is deeper than you think.

you solve one issue to only realize that it wasn't the real issue it was a coping mechanism.

<u>giving 100 percent</u>

you are excited that you have an opportunity of a lifetime, one you would never have again.

you capitalize.

everything is great, you felt that giving 100 is what got you to feel this way.

understand that you only have one, 100.
you have no more.

never give anything a 100% because one wrong move and you will be crushed, somebody else will have that 100 and you will be a zero for a long time.

-a broken but memorable life experience.

<u>reality check III</u>

I let myself slip through the cracks.

-never again

- -

Jupiter

"Our best shot at finding life in our solar system might be to look at the moons of Jupiter…"

Michio Kaku

my unrequited other half.

• • •

we have always spoken about how we were made for each other.

I still believe that one day we will be forced into each other's gravitational pull.

but until then, we will continue to uplift each other in every endeavor.

my love for you is endless.

stay dangerous.

NOTE

Saturn and Uranus have special places in my heart. So impactful that I will not fantasize it with my theme of the universe. It has affected my life so greatly that only my direct feelings could show what I felt.

Make Saturn and Uranus into a universe.
Give it the life that I couldn't.

- -

my dark thoughts are ready to speak.

Saturn

"how rare and beautiful it is to even exist"

Unknown

I don’t know what’s worse

dealing with the lies I’ve told here on Earth or
facing the truth to people who’ve seen me do
them in heaven.

maybe I do need to go to hell.

you try your hardest to reach out so nobody else reaches in.

• • •

when people say,
"What do you need?"

I think to myself,
"How can I say everything without sounding desperate?"

you don't know, so you say nothing.

my emotions are being pulled so many ways that my heart can't take.

I thought I was okay

a note written to myself on August 16, 2018

it's a difference between being dark and cognizant of your situation.

you don't always have to have a smile, you can be content.

I thought I was okay II

a note written to myself on September 2, 2018

at this point in my life, I am doing well, and to say the least, I'm content.

-this is not good, please save me.

I thought I was okay (III)
I realized I wasn't okay
a note written to myself on October 3, 2018

I did not know that me being content with life was just the start of being numb to everything.

I thought it was good to feel nothing, and receive everything, but you have to have an emotion to keep life afloat.

life lesson 4

reality check IV

don’t ask for transparency
but not be transparent
if I fucked up,
let me. the fuck. know.

you know we aren’t progressing
especially due to your passive aggressive bullshit.

-written by a person who is also passive
aggressive

screams are just audible tears that are trying to be
shed.

I wish it was a soundproof room where I could
scream.

my only fear is that those thunderous screams
would turn into an unruly sob.

Uranus

"Uranus is one of the most chaotic and disruptive systems in the solar system"

Mark Showalter

"I have looked further into space than ever human being did before me..."

William Herschel

I couldn't save myself.
here is the aftermath.

my depression is an overarching feeling
that my life is over,
my dreams have been crushed,
and my words are hitting the flames
and the ashes are coating my eye.

just because I am smiling doesn't mean that I am not depressed.

don't confuse my muscle movement for a breakthrough leading me out the darkness, it's just a smile. just a smile. **just. a. smile.**

the fact that a smile can't hold the same meaning at it did, when I was a child, tells you how brutal it truly is

and "it" is fill in the blank, and add whatever currently troubles you.

a fat face, in combination with a big smile, shuts my eyes and locks the tears away.

I put moisturizer on my face, but the tears wipe them off before my washcloth and face cleanser can.

I bet your depressive thoughts can't top mine

• • •

Try me.

horror films depict our worst fears.

I'm living in my own horror film.

my own personal hell.

• • •

I can't eat because my body is filled with regret, bad decisions, and unwanted feelings.

• • •

I have the right to be this sad, but I don't know what is going on with my emotions. I can't control them.

-help, this is scary, I don't know what is happening.

weigh me down so I can have an even disbursement of weight on my body so my pain will not be just on my mind and heart.

it was at this point
where I knew I needed help.

you hit bedrock,
but I'm a little too complex
and rebellious for rock bottom
and you consider doing drugs
honestly,

shit, what else can I lose
what else can be added
to my personal resume of
fuckups, misfortunes,
and horrible life decisions

little did you know, it's a place below rock
bottom called the wasteland.

in the waste land, all that lives there is denial, despair, and you.

you are delusional, and you can't think straight.

you are just trying to figure out every aspect of your life without the valid and actual help of others.

jayceon, please seek help—you need it.

everyone else sits there and watches you struggle. only because you want them to.

the worst part is the wasteland is covered in mirrors, so before others can see that you're struggling you see yourself from every aspect of your life breaking down and not making any more moves till that part of you is doomed and forgotten.

and you can't ask for help, because you can't even mutter the words, and if you did, what would you say?

I'm there, and I have no idea how I'm going to get out.

dreams and nightmares

dreaming is something that I would like to do at night because being awake is a living hell that I continuously have to deal with.

some say nightmares are horrible, but when you live an unbearable life where you never know when shit will hit the fan, knowing that things are going south in a dream leaves you with peace.

when I have a lack of concern and self-respect for myself,

I like it because it makes me

wanted and cared for.

• • •

you are depressed
so, you go to eat
get to the fridge
and there is nothing in there
but butter and a 6-week old pizza
so, you rather drink two bottles of wine
to fill that void,
get tired or horny or both

then that 12 am time turns into
4 am thoughts.

<u>toxic trait 1</u>

adding the grey
when I know it's just
Black
and
white

<u>toxic trait 2</u>

I blame others for not forming habits
when I know I can easily form them myself

<u>toxic trait 3</u>

I don't support myself
because others have not supported me

we don’t let everybody know our truths,
but if they knew I would have to kill myself
before they killed me.

I love myself. I love myself. I love myself.
I love myself. I love myself. I love myself.
I love myself. I love myself. I love myself.
I love myself. I love myself. I love myself.
I love myself. I love myself. I love myself.
I love myself. I love myself. I love myself.
I love myself. I love myself. I love myself.
I love myself. I love myself. I love myself.
I love myself. I love myself. I love myself.
I love myself. I love myself. I love myself.
I love myself. I love myself. I love myself.
I love myself. I love myself. I love myself.
I love myself. I love myself. I love myself.
I love myself. I love myself. I love myself.
I love myself. I love myself. I love myself.
I love myself. I love myself. I love myself.
I love myself. I love myself. I love myself.
I love myself. I love myself. I love myself.
I love myself. I love myself. I love myself.
I love myself. I love myself. I love myself.
I love myself. I love myself. I love myself.
I love myself. I love myself. I love myself.
I love myself. I love myself. I love myself.
I love myself. I love myself. I love myself.
I love myself. I love myself. I love myself.
I love myself. I love myself. I love myself.
I love myself. I love myself. I love myself.
I love myself. I love myself. I love myself.

sometimes you won't believe it,
but it keeps you going.

until next time, dark thoughts

sincerely,

Saturn and Uranus

Neptune and Pluto

"He who is shipwrecked the second time cannot lay the blame on Neptune"

Proverbs

"I was far from you as the Pluto, hidden behind many planets closer to you...You never considered my presence, Yet I'm revolving around seeking just a beam of light from you"

Madhusmita Beura

a song. a wild night. a severed heart.

-the only things they have ever given me

you have shown me that my place in your
universe has had no gravity within your life.

you left a while ago.

it was tragic to see you
but thank you for appearing in my dream

it was detrimental
but you showed me I could dream again.

I thought that I pushed you away or
that I was intrusive and abrasive

I used to check in on you to see if you were okay

you had me question my ability to care for others,
and had me wondering if I should even do it.

through our separation, I realized that I am a
gem, and we all need somebody to reach out and
check on us.

just because you put me on DND does not mean
that I should stop looking out for people I care
about.

I just have to be more careful about who I choose
to lookout for

I miss and love you
but I don’t wish you the best.

museum I

you have created a crater in my life that I have
not had filled yet.

my body has not been repurposed. it has only
been used as a museum that other planets study
and revolve around in awe.

they wonder what happen.

and like a planet that is hit by a comet,
they don't even know—
they just know it happened.

they study its body to figure out the cause.

they only know that this extraterrestrial body
came into their atmosphere, and they only hoped
that it would land in the ocean creating
earthquakes and fucking up the ocean floor.

museum II

instead it hit the mainland and killed civilians.

they were not ready for you.
I was not ready for you.

you came and destroyed others. your body was a sight and a site of interest because we did not know you were capable of this type of destruction.

you were destroyed and you left an unhealable blemish on the face of the Earth.

as the Earth fills itself in and tries to create life in that spot, it will always know that something tragic happened there.

as you sit in the museum,
glorified for your unintentional devastation.

I do not need to seek revenge, because I know
you all are dealing with your own battles

-growth

shitty love life

to the girl that I once affinitied

I told you that my biggest fear was being loved.
to that, you had no emotion or movement.
you hit me with, "that was deep"

I felt that I was getting somewhere

I wasn't

"that was deep" was the farthest I would ever get with her.

she took my biggest fear, and me liking her, and threw it back at me

with no remorse

I couldn't even be mad at her because my inner conscience knew the brutal reality that lied behind the confident, cocky phase.

for the other one:

one day, I was reading a journal entry I wrote
about you from years ago.

a few days later, I saw you

gave you a hug, said goodbye

hoping that you would ask for my number again
(hoping you didn't even delete it) or "you tryna
hang?"

didn't get that

but it's great to know you're doing well

Love,

jayceon

you have all shown me life lessons.
thank you.

Unnamed Stars

"The unnamed should not be mistaken for nonexistent"

Catharine MacKinnon

this is for every star that I have glanced and admired but have not had the time to name. you have impacted my life, only for the better. and to this, I give you not only a piece in my heart, but the universe.

may your eternal glow,
forever light the world.

a few gems for the road. (to the reader)

I used to think that I was not able to connect
with everyone

because I can't…

I will never be everyone's cup of tea

honestly, some of y'all can't handle the heat, and I
drink more than black tea, so be ready for my
dynamic.

gems II

to you all:
I am a bad bitch
I used to think I was unattractive

this has allowed me not to have confidence

I am no longer going to destroy myself for things
that I cannot change

and things that don't need to be changed

do the same

be a bad bitch all summer, winter, fall, and spring
20xx

cause, baby, if nobody tells you this

YOU ARE THE BADDEST HUMAN
ORBITING THE SUN

shine, sis.

gems III

right now, you won't know

that has to be the beauty in your situation

the beauty that anything and everything will
happen to make you the person that you were
meant to be.

-a boy in distress

gems IV

don’t send me a playlist and expect us not to discuss it

best believe that, baby

gems V

too often we say,
"if they can do it, I can"

start saying,
"if I can do it, I will"

gems VI

some demons will never have the time of day

some demons will be present here and there

some demons will be the only thing that will make your life interesting. They feed off of your fears in hopes it will overtake you.

—it won't, trust me

gems VII

as you search for love

remember. you are an experience.

your words
your values
your opinions
your beauty
your faults
your cracks

and

your dreams

are all intertwined and anyone who only seeks one does not deserve to be blessed by your wonderful creation.

seek someone who is willing to experience you
all of you

it is here that I say my final goodbyes.

I hope you learned as much as I did.

Thank you.

You have traveled the galaxy with me over these 166 pages and these 5,849 words. I am blessed to share my worldly perspective of conversations and thoughts that are near and dear to my heart.

I hope that you all have defined the parameters of your own galaxy.

Remember that stars and planets only help to enhance your galaxy, but be able to understand the thin line between enhancement and abuse.

Until next time,

If nobody else does,
I'll love you to the moon back.

The light you have given to this dark universe will travel to the ends of it until that is the only substance it is made up of.

Love,

Jayceon

dealing. (my final, final words)

I have been dealing for the past 19 years
i'm ready to sit down,
take the risk,
and,
play the game

You got next?

Made in the
USA
Lexington, KY